Signs Along t

D0127458

Learning to Read the Natural Landscape

written and illustrated by Kayo Robertson

o:
meadow
t you've already
en the
igns along
he River"
m your
Raft!

ROBERTS RINEHART, INC. PUBLISHERS

Love,

Cascade + Jayleen

To Gwen, who opened the first pages . . .

Published by Roberts Rinehart, Inc. Publishers
P.O. Box 3161 Boulder, Colorado 80303
International Standard Book Number 0-911797-22-x
Library of Congress Catalog Card Number 85-63524
Printed in the United States of America

About the Plates that Follow

Nature doesn't often shout its story; the landscape reveals itself to us silently and with subtlety. Thus in the succeeding pages I have chosen to leave parts of the story unspoken. It has been my experience that Albert Einstein's belief — "imagination is more important than knowledge" — can be applied to introducing nature to children. Nothing stifles the learning process more than telling too much of the story. Allowed to follow their own native curiosity, to wonder, to question, and even to reach the wrong conclusion now and then, children begin to develop a process of inquiry. Far more meaningful than rote recitations of scientific data, this spirit of inquiry will put the breath of life into knowledge.

This process will naturally lead to more questions than answers. In order to come to the aid of parents, teachers, and beginning naturalists, I have provided a separate guide to each of the plates that starts on page 54. Here one may learn a bit more about the plants and animals depicted on these pages, as well as their role in the natural life of a river's ecosystem.

LONG AGO, before the time of books, people read the signs of nature. A track, the gnawings on a twig, or some bent grasses each told a story. If you look, you too can learn to read these signs and a whole new world will open. Just like the pages of a book . . .

Empty skins on rocks and grasses tell a story of water insects growing up.

Dimples on the water tell of feeding trout.

There are signs you can see.

Tracks in the mud might tell a story of a moonlit fisherman.

There are signs you can smell.

Some signs, like the music of wild geese,

you can hear.

A few chewed blades of grass . . .

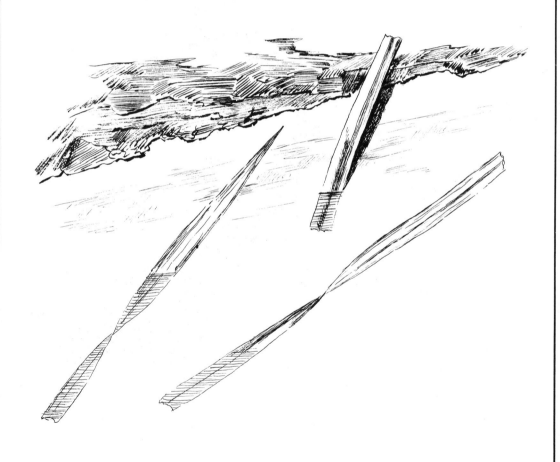

A feather on the water . . .

Some old bones along the bank . . .

. . . all tell a story.

This fallen antler

tells a story . . .

. . . of the elk

that shed it . . .

. . . and a wandering porcupine that gnawed upon it.

Some signs are as old as the rocks themselves.

Others are as new as a day-old fawn.

Each sign has its season,

each season its sign.

Winter's bare branches

tell of last spring's birds.

Fresh snow is like a new page.

Snowmelt reveals yet more signs, such as pocket gopher mounds.

Gopher diggings tell of tasty roots.

Badger diggings tell of tasty gophers.

What goes into an animal

must come out.

You can find mouse bones in coyote scat.

Deer Sign.

Bird scat that you can spot on rock cliffs is called "white wash."

There you know large birds

have waited and watched.

Each creature writes its
story upon the landscape.

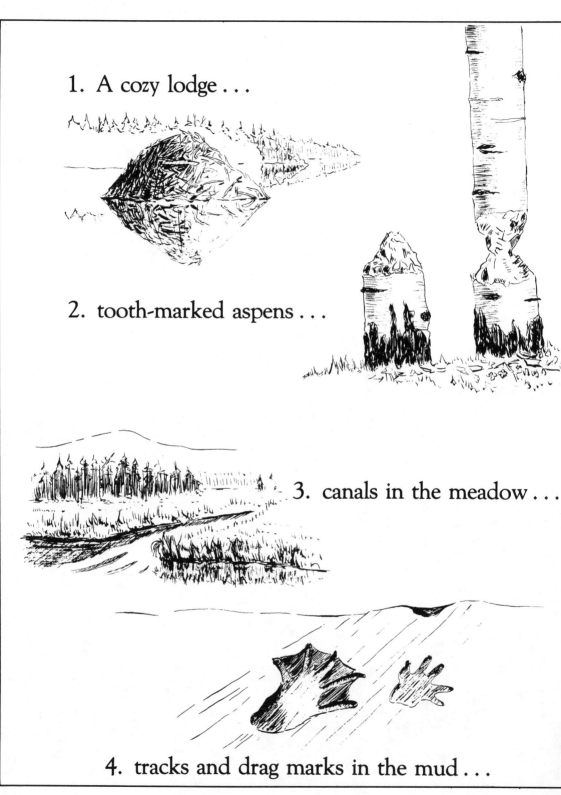

1. A cozy lodge . . .

2. tooth-marked aspens . . .

3. canals in the meadow . . .

4. tracks and drag marks in the mud . . .

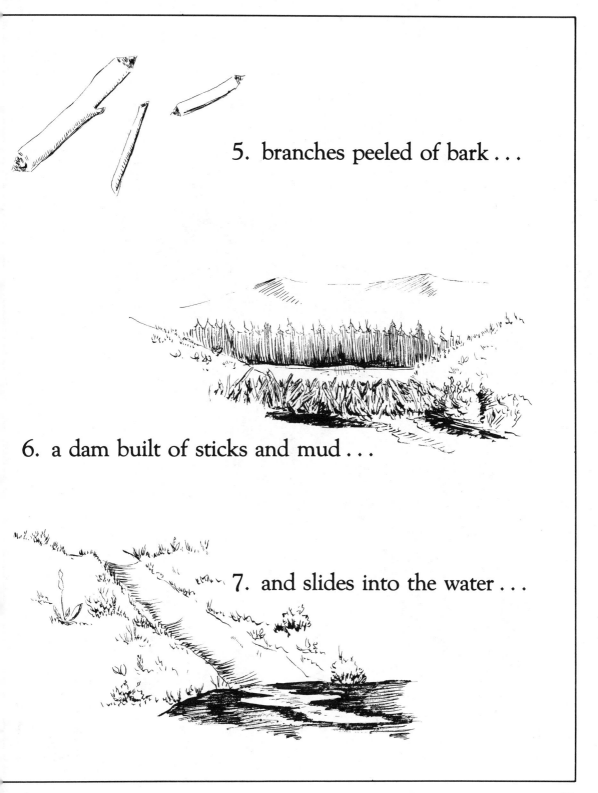

5. branches peeled of bark . . .

6. a dam built of sticks and mud . . .

7. and slides into the water . . .

. . . all spell "beaver."

These signs spell bear.

claw marks

overturned rocks and logs

tracks

Gnawed branches are stories written by teeth.

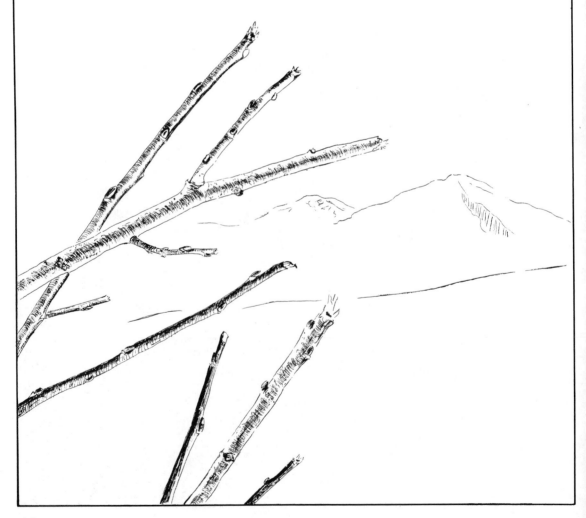

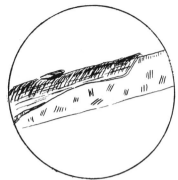

They can tell tales of mice or moose.

Thousands of animal signs surround us.

Learn to read them letter by letter,

word by word,

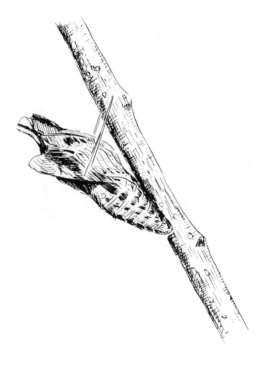

until a story unfolds.

Down by the river is an open book . . .

Afterword

Ecology begins at home, and the best place to learn to read nature's language is your own back yard. Continue your explorations with journeys to your local nature center, wildlife refuge, wilderness area, state or national park. Park naturalists, biologists, teachers, hunters, fishermen, trappers, and museums and libraries are but a few of the resources available to help you.

Life on earth is a vast, woven fabric of which we humans are but a single strand. To study nature is to become aware of the patterns, colors, forms, beauty, and integrity of the entire fabric. It not only adds to the richness of our lives, but also brings us to an appreciation of how each strand combines to strengthen and support the whole.

List of Plates

12-13 Animal signs are not always spectacular. A few blades of neatly cut grass floating in the water often mean that a family of muskrats lives close by.

14-15 Animals are constantly shedding fur and feathers. With practice and experience these are easy to read. This dotted breast feather tells of a blue-winged teal.

16-17 Wild creatures don't always have the best table manners. After supper there are usually enough scraps left behind to tell the story. These sucker remains tell a tale of another large fishing bird, the bald eagle.

18-20 Like the chapters of an unfolding book, there are stories within stories. These antlers, now overgrown by a carpet of columbine and wild geranium, tell of late winter when a large bull elk shed the headress that had served him in love and war the previous autumn. Like all male members of the deer family, elk grow new antlers each spring. Antlers are used to attract females and intimidate rival males during an autumn mating season known as the rut.

The antlers also tell of a gnawing animal, a rodent. Porcupines, which feed mainly on bark, find shed antlers a favorite source of minerals.

21 The form and nature of the land itself — rocks, soil, valleys, fossils, lakes, mountains, and rivers — tell the oldest tales. Those who can read these stories are called geologists. This fossil fish tells of life in an ancient, inland, freshwater sea.

22-23 Throughout the world, the comings and goings of plants and animals are marked by the changing seasons of the temperate climes. Birthing and dying both march to this timeless rhythm. Pictured here are the springborn fawn of a deer nestled in a bed of avalanche lilies, and a flurry of windblown autumn leaves.

24-25 Winter is a quiet time, yet signs of wildlife are everywhere. As cold winds wash the leaves from the trees, bird nests, once hidden in summer greenery, become obvious. Look for the bulky, domed nests of magpies in the boughs of cottonwood trees. Equipped with both front and rear entrances, the cozy nests provide protection from sun and cold, wind and predators.

26-30   Some of the best wildlife stories are both written and read on the pages of newly fallen snow. The tracks of a cottontail rabbit are here joined with the wingprints of one of nature's fiercest hunters, the golden eagle.

In order to live all animals must eat. Animals that kill and eat other animals are called predators. The animals they eat are called prey.

31-32   For many creatures snow means the protection of a roof overhead. Not until spring do the winter burrows, runways, and nests of mice, voles, and gophers appear. Pocket gophers dig tunnels in the snow which they fill with dirt from their many underground excavations. As the snow melts these ribbons of dirt are laid gently upon the ground.

33   Where there is gopher sign one will usually find the sign of gopher hunters. Badgers often hunt by digging right into the homes of gophers, mice, and ground squirrels.

34   Using the sun's energy to combine elements of the soil, air, and water, plants are uniquely able to create their own food. This marvelous process is known as photosynthesis (literally "to put together with light").

As animals eat plants and in turn are eaten by other animals, what we call a "food chain" is produced. In this fashion nutrients move from the earth to plants, from the eaters of plants (herbivores) to the eaters of meat (carnivores) and ultimately back to the earth in a never-ending cycle.

The energy in this lupine pod travels through a deer mouse and a coyote before once again fertilizing plants in the form of coyote scat.

35-36   Scats are excellent evidence that an animal has been in the vicinity. Bones, berries, seeds, feathers, and fur found in animal scat, along with the shape and location of the scat itself, are all clues that tell a story. Fat mice make contented coyotes.

37   These firm, slightly elongated, pellet-like scats along with the heart-shaped, pointed hoof prints belong to a mule deer buck.

38-39   While smaller songbirds usually hide their scat as well as that of their young to avoid detection, the larger raptors (hunters, birds of prey) have no need to be so careful. Their nesting and roosting sites are often easily discovered by watching for telltale "whitewash."

With its uncanny senses of sight and hearing and formidable talons, the great horned owl, like the golden eagle, has little to fear from other predators.

40-41   Animals that tend to stay near a centrally located homesite, such as the beaver, often leave many easy-to-read signs.

42-43   1. The cone-shaped beaver lodge is home for the whole beaver family. It can be built into a river bank or in the middle of a pond created by the beaver themselves. The entrance is usually under water. Like all homes, it provides warmth, comfort, and safety.
2. Aspen is a favorite tree of the beaver clan. They eat the bark and twigs and build dams and lodges with the branches.
3. Beaver must often haul logs from a great distance. Canals dug adjacent to their ponds allow the beaver to float heavy logs into position and thus avoid the tedious labor of dragging.
4. The large, webbed, five-toed tracks, along with drag marks made by the beaver's tail or the branches it might haul, are both characteristic signs.
5. Beaver chop and store branches for their winter food supply. A tooth-marked branch, cleaned of bark and floating in the water, generally means a beaver lives upstream.
6. Beaver are superb engineers, able to dam streams and some rivers. The activities of every living thing affects in a great or small way every other living thing. A beaver dam creates a pond which acts as a moat of safety around the beaver's lodge. The pond also provides a home for ducks, muskrats, mink, fishes, frogs, and other creatures. A web of relationships is thus created between the beaver and many other creatures, their predators, prey, and parasites. The study of these complex webs of relationships is called ecology.
7. Where it is impossible to build a canal, beaver will make slides to ease the job of hauling logs to their pond.

44   Beaver may best be observed by quietly sitting near their pond at dawn or dusk. The large paddle-shaped tail not only helps a beaver to swim and stand but also can make a loud booming splash on the water's surface to warn other beaver that danger is nearby.

45   Like many "nocturnal" animals — those that work mostly at night — black bears are seldom seen but leave many signs. In bear country mud wallows, tracks, scat, claw marks, hair stuck in the bark of "rubbing trees," torn-up anthills, and rocks and logs overturned for the tasty insects underneath them are a few such signs.

46-47   Many creatures besides beaver feed on twigs and bark. Clues as to the kind of creature can be found in the size of toothmarks, the kind of tree or shrub, the season in which the mark was made, and the height of the mark (remember, mice can climb and rabbits can stand on the snow). Rodents and rabbits tend to leave neatly incised toothmarks while larger ungulates (animals with hooves) leave ragged twig ends. In the winter some creatures such as this moose feed almost entirely on twigs, in this case the twigs of a willow.

48-50   Since insects are among the most prolific creatures on earth, it is only natural that their sign should be everywhere. Eggs, cuttings, nests, and skins can all be found with but a little searching.

   All insects, such as this tiger swallowtail butterfly, live their lives in stages. In the case of the swallowtail, one stage hardly resembles the next. The swallowtail larva or caterpillar might be tracked down by circular cuts in wild cherry leaves, the pupa hidden away in a tight chrysalis, while the adult butterfly will follow the scents of summer flowers.

51   As we become better able to read nature's signs, the land becomes more and more our home, its creatures more and more our neighbors. As we come to understand how our fellow species live, we in turn become better neighbors. One sign leads to the next and before we know it we find ourselves on an incredible adventure of discovery.

52   We share this adventure with all living things, for in its own way each creature learns to read the world that surrounds it.

   Here a coyote reads a story of hunter and hunted — moccasin and deer prints.

Field Notes

golden-mantled ground squirrel

Field Notes

California poppy